8　9　10　TEN TIMES TEN

To the Teachers
and
Especially
Virginie

English edition first published 2014 by order of the Tate Trustees
by Tate Publishing, a division of Tate Enterprises Ltd,
Millbank, London SW1P 4RG
www.tate.org.uk/publishing

This edition © Tate 2014

First published in French as *Dix Fois Dix* © Editions du Seuil, 2003 for the
first edition; © Editions du Seuil, 2013 for this edition

A catalogue record for this book is available from the British Library
ISBN 978 1 84976 247 2
Distributed in the United States and Canada by ABRAMS, New York
Library of Congress Control Number applied for
Printed in France

10 times 10

TATE PUBLISHING

TABLE OF CONTENTS

 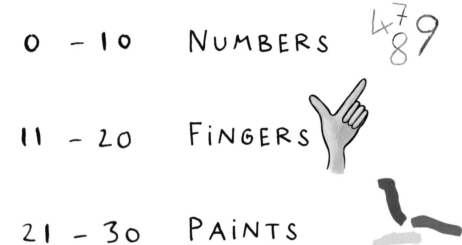

AND FINALLY

Numbers

0

ZERO

ONE

TWO

THREE

4

FOUR

5

FiVE

6

six

7

SEVEN

8

EiGHT

NINE

9

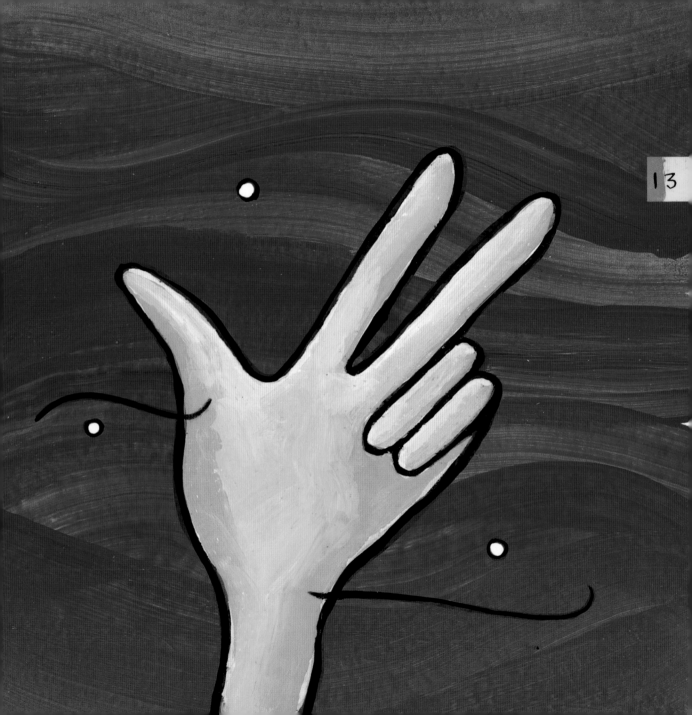

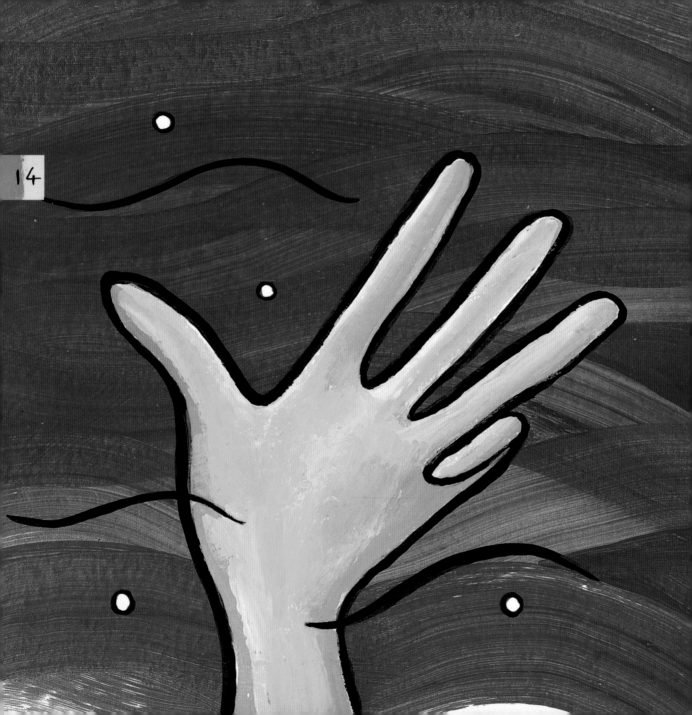

15

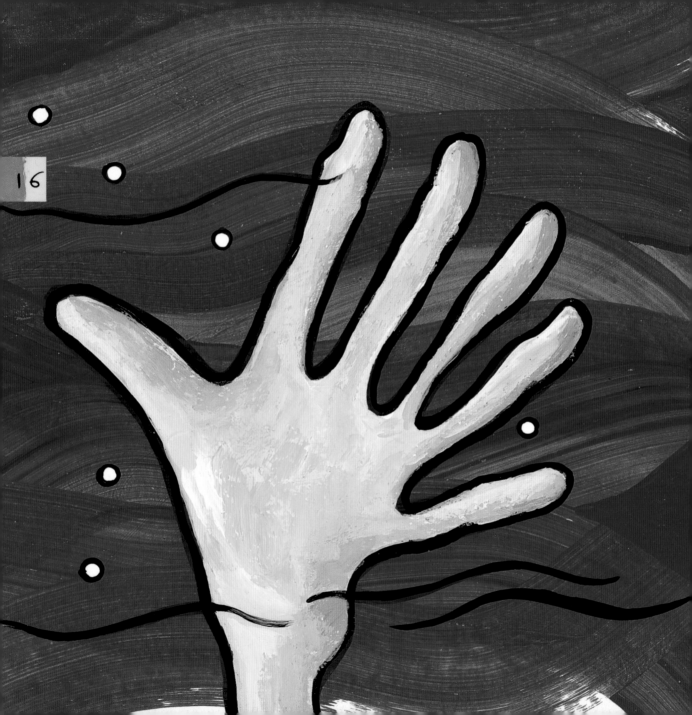

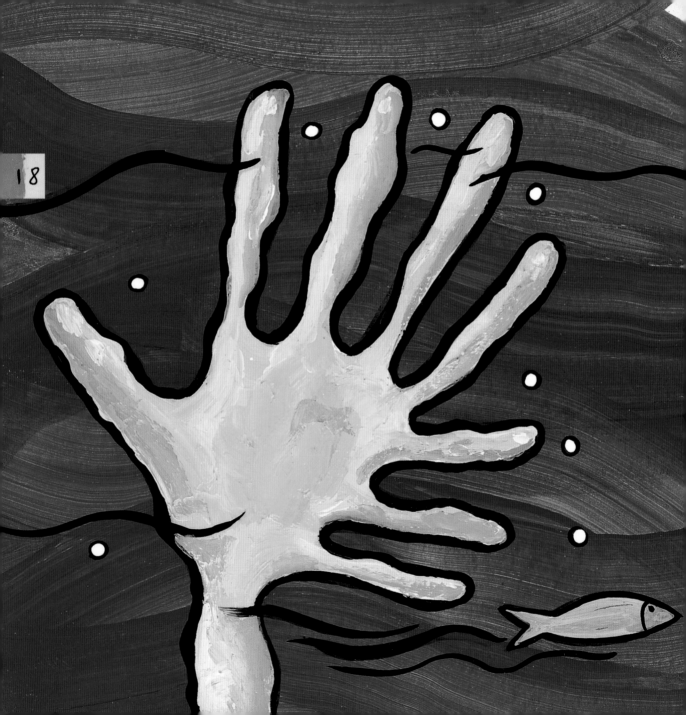

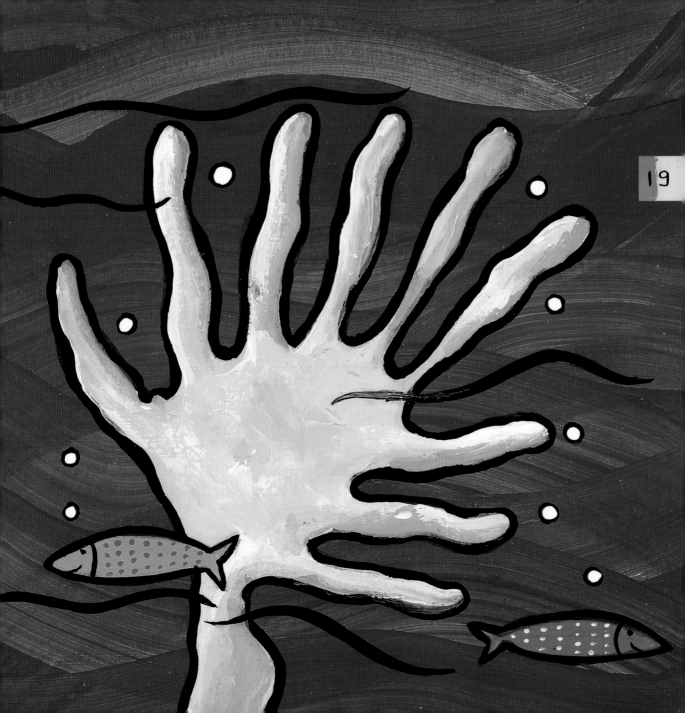

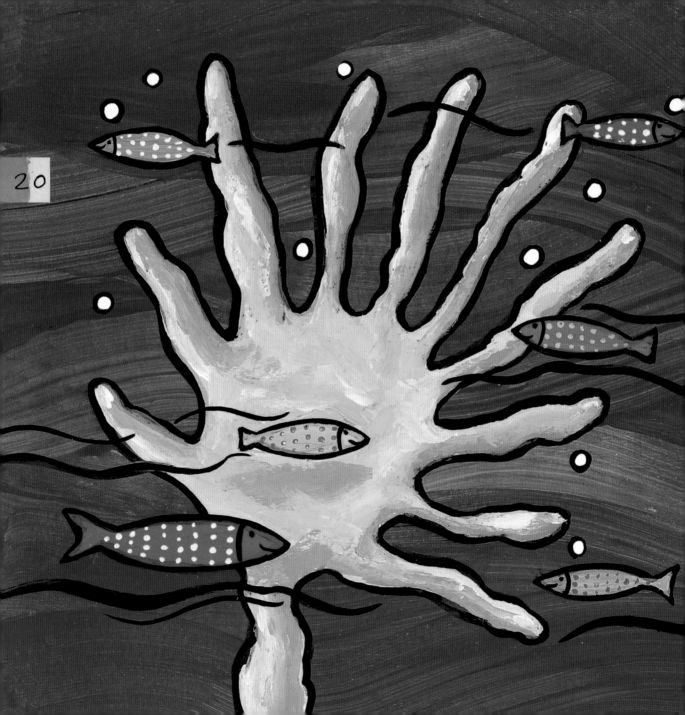

20

21

ONE IS WHITE.

TWO IS RED.

23

THREE iS YELLOW.

FOUR IS BLUE.

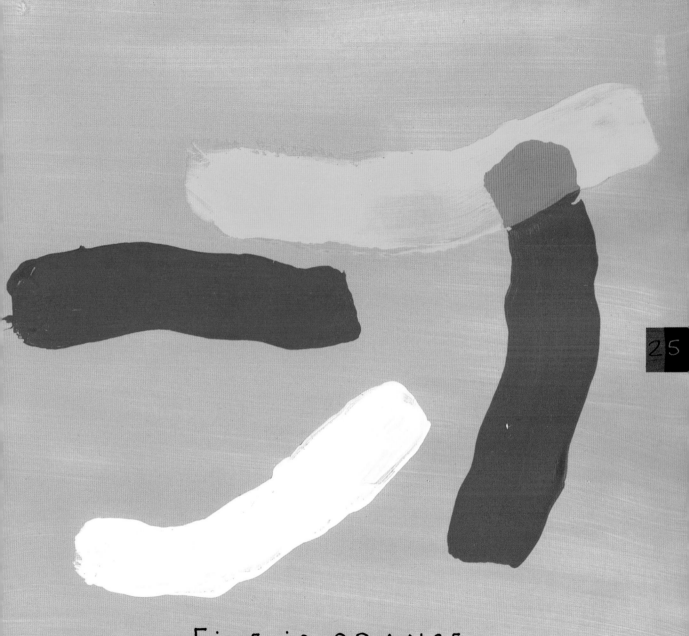

FIVE IS ORANGE.

25

26

Six is GREEN.

27

SEVEN IS PINK.

28

EIGHT IS PURPLE.

29

NINE IS BROWN.

30

TEN IS BLACK.

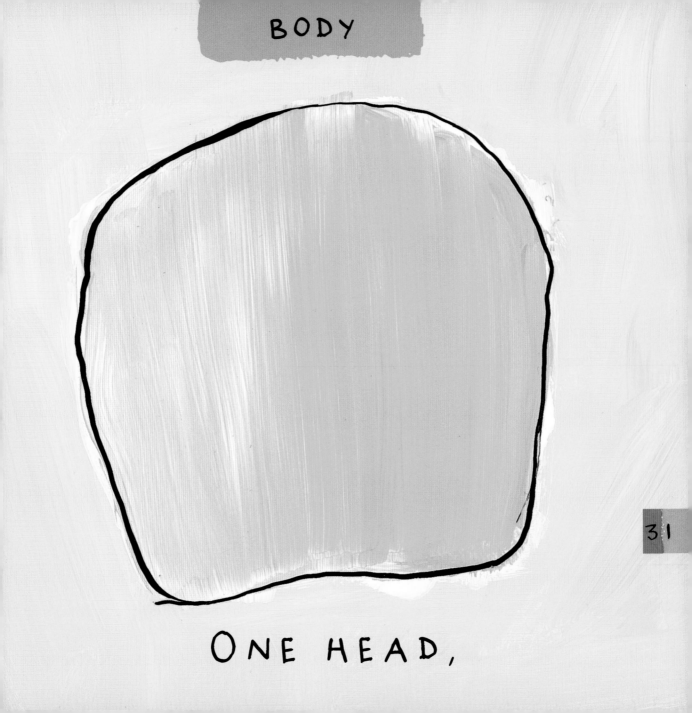

31

ONE HEAD,

TWO EARS,

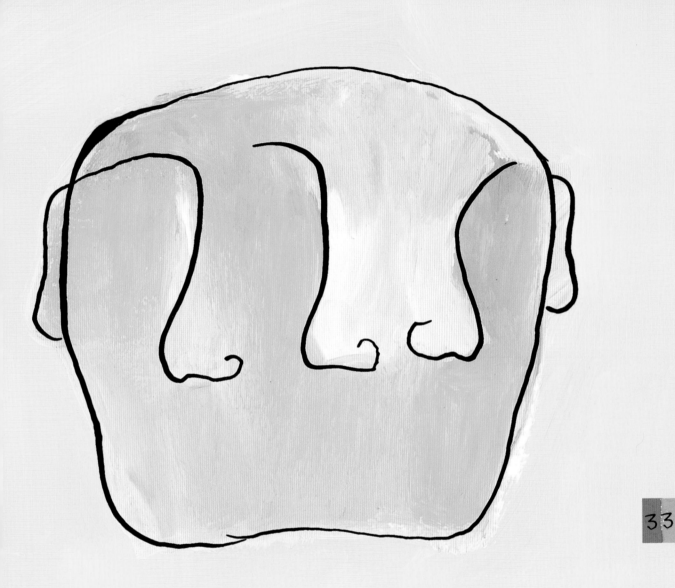

THREE NOSES,

FOUR EYES,

FIVE MOUTHS,

35

Six FEET,

SEVEN ARMS,

EiGHT NOSTRiLS,

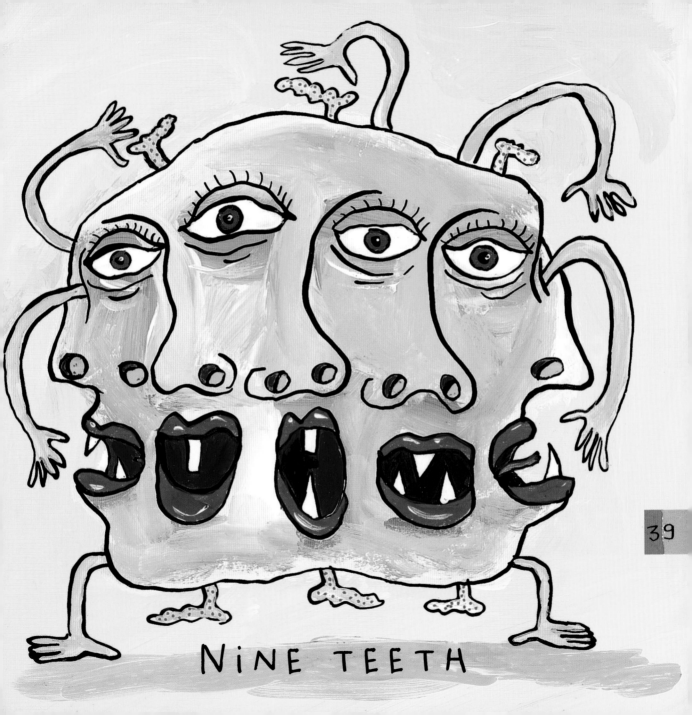

NiNE TEETH

39

AND TEN HAIRS.

CREATION

42

45

47

49

50

52

54

55

57

60

70

ONE CASTLE, WHERE ONCE UPON A TIME
THERE LIVED...

TWO HANDSOME PRINCES

AND THREE BEAUTiFUL PRiNCESSES.

SUDDENLY, FOUR CRUEL WITCHES CAST A
SPELL THAT TURNED THEM ALL INTO

FIVE CROAKING FROGS.

75

FORTUNATELY, SIX KIND FAIRIES REMOVED THE SPELL

FROM THE SEVEN POISONED APPLES,

78

AND NiNE KiSSES OF TRUE LOVE.

79

TEN CHILDREN WERE BORN TO THE
HAPPY ROYALS.

80

AND THEY ALL LIVED
HAPPILY EVER AFTER!

81

82

83

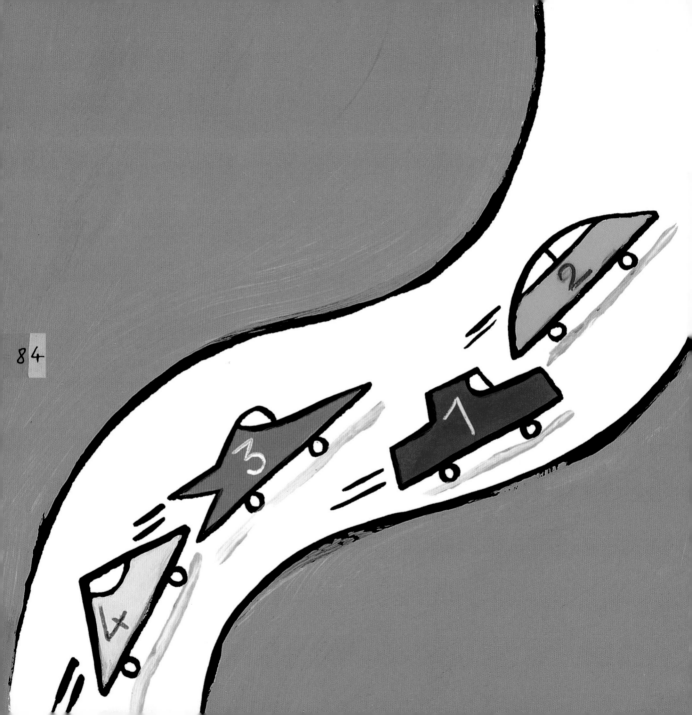

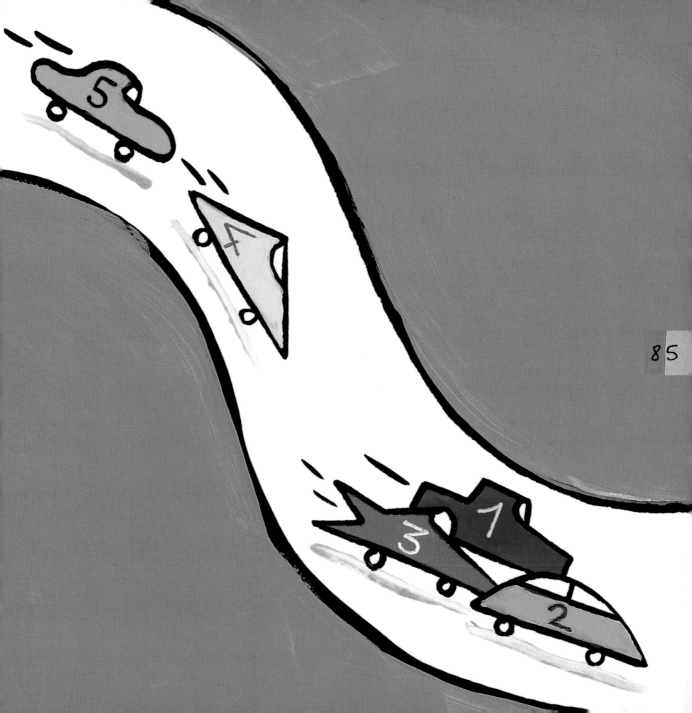

85

86

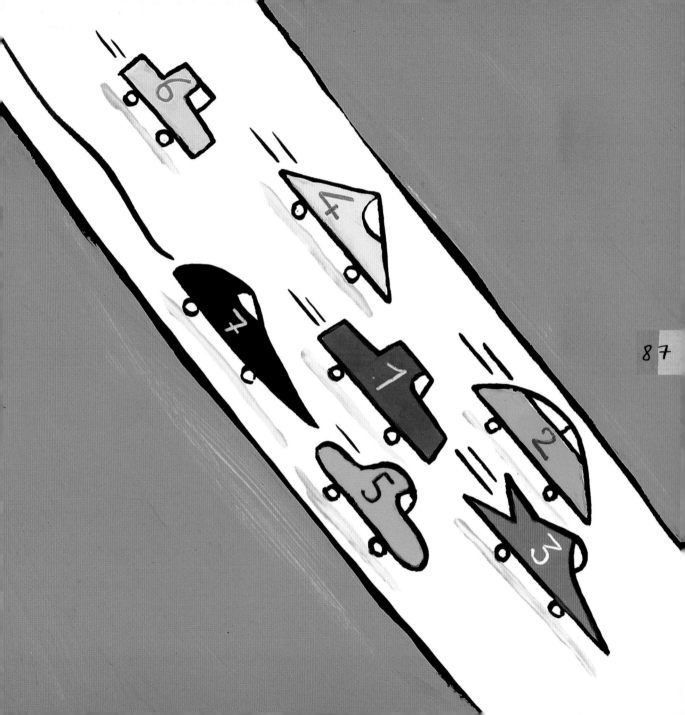

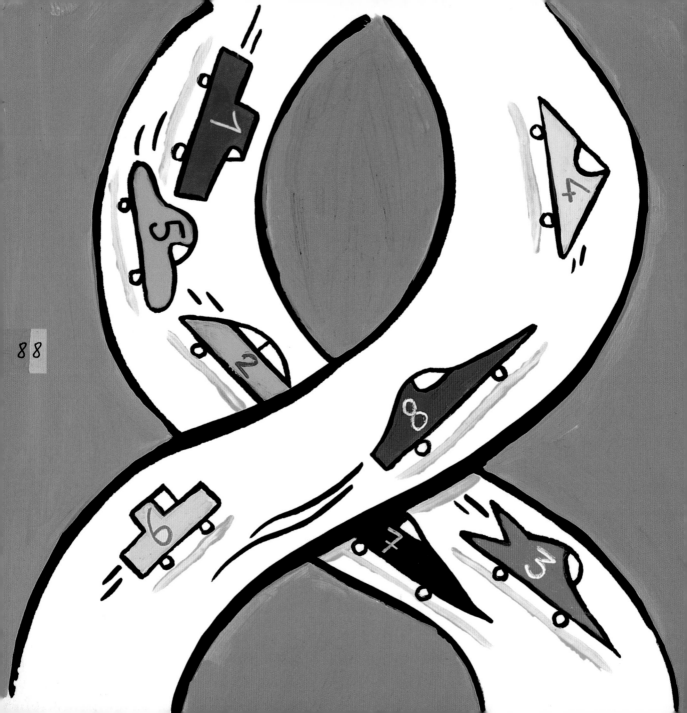

89

ONE ANIMAL?

9

THREE HEARTS?

93

FOUR LEGS?

Six hours?

EIGHT PIECES?

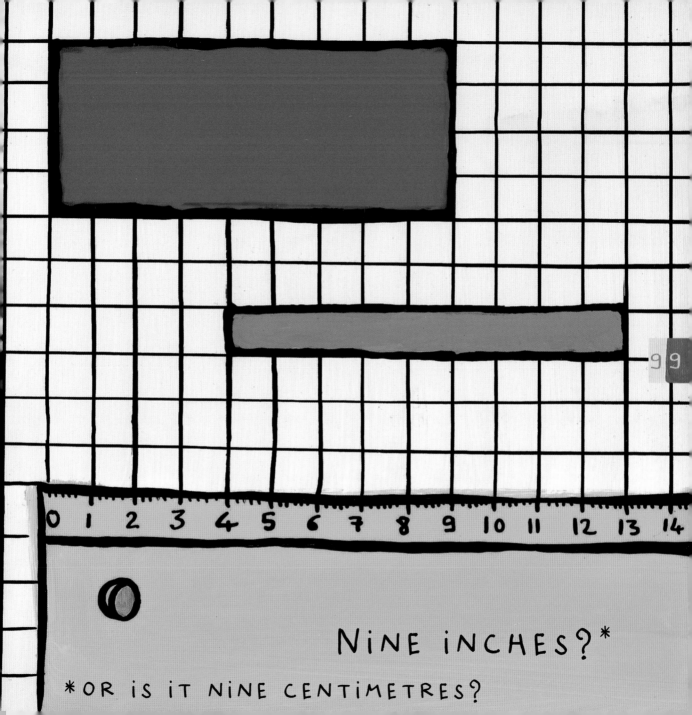

99

0 1 2 3 4 5 6 7 8 9 10 11 12 13 14

NINE INCHES?*

*OR IS IT NINE CENTIMETRES?

TEN POINTS?

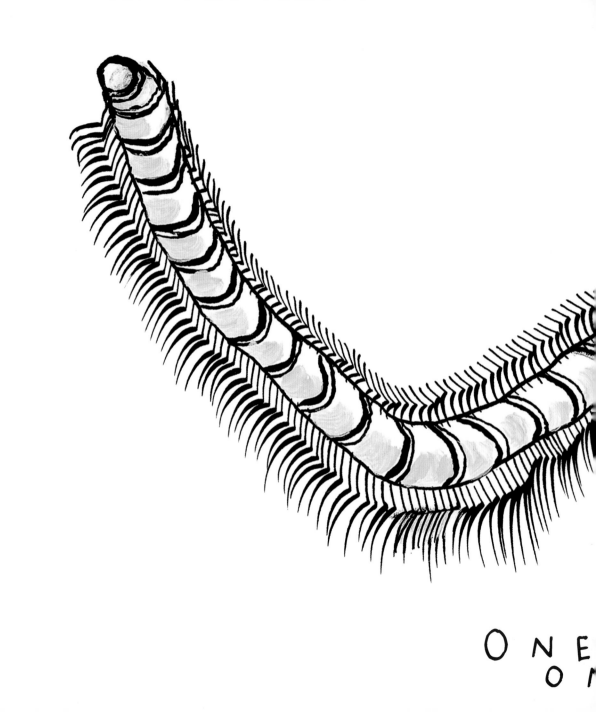

O N E

O N

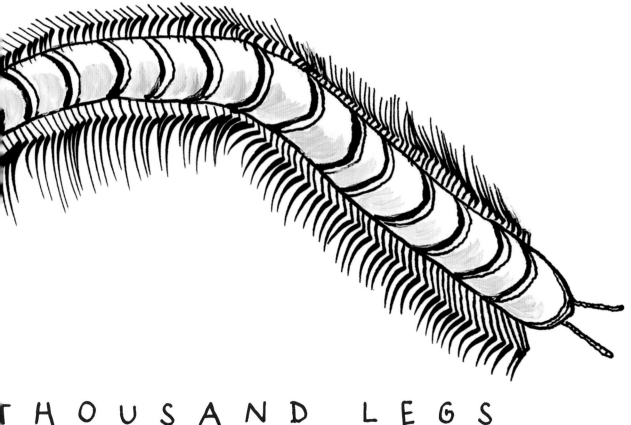

THOUSAND LEGS
A MiLLiPEDE.

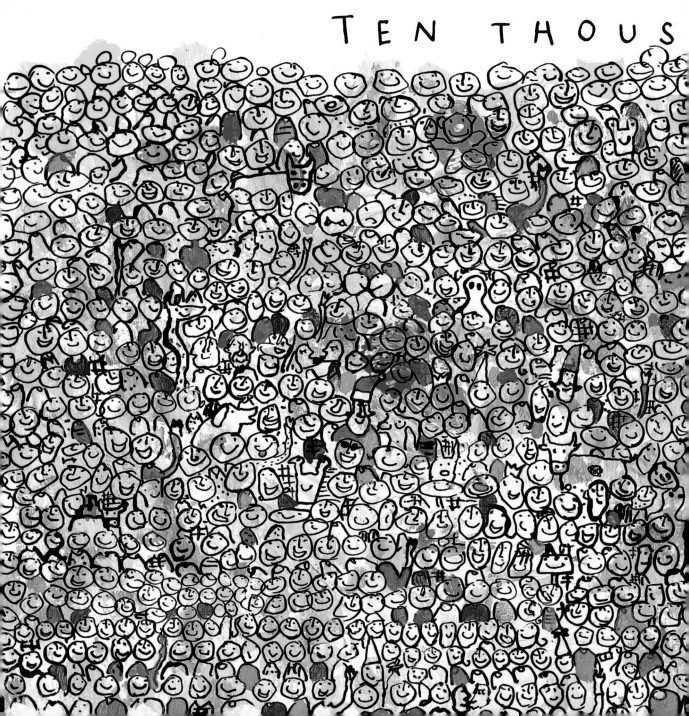

ONE THOUSAND MI

iON GRAINS OF SAND.

ONE THOUSAND Bi

ION STARS.

AND MORE,

ALSO BY HERVÉ TULLET FROM TATE PUBLISHING:

THE FIVE SENSES

THE SCRIBBLE BOOK

THE COLOURING BOOK

THE BOOK WITH A HOLE